The Three SILLY Billies

To my one and only "Groucho"—*M. P.*

For my buddies Theo and Zach—*B. M.*

SIMON & SCHUSTER BOOKS FOR YOUNG READERS
An imprint of Simon & Schuster Children's Publishing Division
1230 Avenue of the Americas, New York, New York 10020
Text copyright © 2005 by Margie Palatini
Illustrations copyright © 2005 by Barry Moser
SIMON & SCHUSTER BOOKS FOR YOUNG READERS is a trademark of Simon & Schuster, Inc.
Book design by Mark Siegel
The text for this book is set in Garamond.
The illustrations for this book are rendered in transparent watercolor on handmade Italian paper.
Manufactured in China
10 9 8 7 6 5 4 3
Library of Congress Cataloging-in-Publication Data
Palatini, Margie.
The three silly billies / Margie Palatini ; illustrated by Barry Moser.
p. cm.
Summary: Three billy goats, unable to cross a bridge because they cannot pay the toll, form a car pool with the Three Bears, Little Red Riding Hood, and Jack of beanstalk fame to get past the rude Troll.
ISBN 0-689-85862-0 (Hardcover)
[1. Characters in literature—Fiction. 2. Humorous stories.] I. Moser, Barry, ill. II. Title.
PZ7.P1755 Th 2005
[E]—dc21   2002155835

The **SILLY**

Three
Billies

by *Margie Palatini*
Illustrated by *Barry Moser*

Simon & Schuster Books for Young Readers
New York   London   Toronto   Sydney

The Three Silly Billies were ready to kick up their heels and have some fun in the sun. They packed up their old jalopy, and with a spit, a chug, and a honk, off they tootled. Down the hill and through the woods went the billies until they came to a small wooden bridge that crossed a very deep river.

CLACKETY CLACK. CLACKETY CLACK. CLACKETY CLACK.

"Who's crossing my bridge?" shouted a grumpy, stumpy little man who was blocking their path.

"We're the billies. Billy Bob, Billy Bo, and Just Plain Billy," explained the biggest billy, who was Bob. "We're revved up and ready to roll!"

"Hold your horsepower," said the little man with a stamp, a stomp, and a snort. "This is a troll bridge. I'm the Troll. Now, start passing the buck."

"A buck?" said Just Plain Billy. "But that's four quarters. Ten dimes. Twenty nickels. A hundred pennies. That's one whole dollar!"

"This isn't a freeway," said the greedy, grumpy little man. "Just show me the money!"

Billy Bob had thirty cents. Billy Bo had twenty cents. As usual, Just Plain Billy had no cents at all. No matter how they added it up, the Three Silly Billies did not have enough money to pay the Troll.

But the middle billy, who was Bo, had an idea. "What we need is—a car pool! We can share the fare!"

So Billy Bob opened the trunk. Billy Bo pumped up the pool. And Just Plain Billy fetched some pails of water. With a *splish,* a *splash,* and a *slosh,* the Three Silly Billies grabbed their rubber duckies and jumped into their car pool. "We'll just wade and wait for someone to jump in and join us," said Billy Bo with a bob.

The Troll grumbled, "Crazy kids." He shook his head at their silliness and stomped back to his troll booth.

And then . . .

CLACKETY CLACK. CLACKETY CLACK. CLACKETY CLACK.

"Who's crossing my bridge?" shouted the Troll.

"It's just us. The Three Bears from the other side of the river," answered the big papa bear. "We're taking a walk through the woods before dinner."

"Lookee here, Teddy," said the little man with a stamp, a stomp, and a snort. "All you'll be eating is dust from 'detour du jour' unless you start coughing up some coins."

"Oh, dear," said Papa Bear, looking in his wallet. "I only have one thin dime."

"Oh, my," said Mama Bear, peeking into her purse. "I only have one wooden nickel."

Baby Bear cried, "Don't count on me. I don't even get an allowance."

The Troll grunted. "Then take a hike."

Mama Bear fretted. "What ever will we do? If we don't get home soon, our porridge will be cold."

"And I hate cold porridge," said Papa Bear with a worried sigh.

"Why not add your money to our money?" blurted out Billy Bob. "Join our car pool so we can cross the bridge together."

"Makes a lot of cents to me," said Baby Bear. "Where are my water wings?"

So Billy Bob added up the moolah. Billy Bo held out the pot. And Papa, Mama, and Little Baby Bear jumped feet first into the car pool.

The water was just right.

"I still say that idea is all wet," mumbled the Troll. He shook his head at their silliness and stomped back to his troll booth.

And then . . .

CLACKETY CLACK. CLACKETY CLACK. CLACKETY CLACK.

"Who's crossing my bridge?" shouted the Troll.

"It's only me, Little Red Riding Hood. I'm on my way to Grandma's house."

"Well, you can kiss seeing your granny good-bye unless you have a bill in that basket, missy," said the little man with a stamp, a stomp, and a snort. "Can't you see the sign?"

"Oh my goodness! What a big toll you have!" sighed Little Red Riding Hood.

But all Little Red Riding Hood could find in her basket was one crummy quarter, a gooey nickel, and three sticky pennies.

"Hey, Red, don't be blue," called out Billy Bob. "Pool your resources with ours so we can cross the bridge together."

"Count me in," said Little Red, making a big splash.

"Pitiful party animals," grumbled the Troll. He shook his head at their silliness and stomped back to his troll booth.

And then . . .

CLACKETY CLACK. CLACKETY CLACK. CLACKETY CLACK.

"Who's crossing my bridge?" shouted the Troll.

"It's just Jack. I'm bringing my poor mother some magic beans I traded for our cow."

"Beans? You need a reality check, junior," said the little man with a stamp, a stomp, and a snort.

The boy held out his hand. "But all I have left are these beans and two pennies."

"Then hit the road, Jack!" shouted the Troll, spilling the beans into the river.

Poor Jack didn't have a clue what to do.

"Don't worry, kiddo," called out Billy Bo. "Put in your two cents over here."

So, *splish splash,* in jumped Jack, who plunked down his pennies and topped off the pot.

The Troll stamped and stomped. He stormed and stewed. He snorted and cavorted until he was blue in the face.

"I want my money, you four-legged buttinskis!" he shouted, tramping up to the car pool. "Give it to me now! Now! Now!"

Mama Bear raised an eyebrow at such behavior. "You know, my little fellow, I think you deserve everything that's coming to you."

The Troll snorted. "So let me have it!"

Billy Bob looked at Billy Bo, who gave a nod to Just Plain Billy, who pulled the plug. "Everybody out of the pool!"

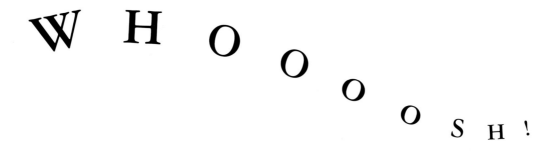

WHOOOOOOSH!

"Man overboard!" called out Billy Bob, tossing the Troll a spare tire.

And as the grumpy, greedy little man glugged and gulped, Jack, Red, Papa, Mama, and Little Baby Bear waved good-bye, and floated safely across to the other side of the river . . . where they hurried home to meet their mother, visit Granny, and eat their porridge.

The Three Silly Billies turned over the pot and dropped every last penny, nickel, dime, and quarter into the Troll's troll booth. *Plink. Plunk. Clink. Clink. Clunk.* Exactly one dollar.

And across the small wooden bridge that crossed the very deep river, went the Three Silly Billies for some fun in the sun.

Which would be the end—but then . . .

CLACKETY CLACK. CLACKETY CLACK. CLACKETY CLACK.

"Oh, who's crossing my bridge now?" grumbled the Troll with a soggy sigh and a gurgle.

"Just little ol' me," bellowed the Giant with a sniff. "Fee fie fo fum . . . Is that a troll I smell? . . . Yummy yum yum!"